The Adirondack Kids™ #3

The Lost Lighthouse

by Justin & Gary VanRiper
Illustrations by Glenn Guy

Adirondack Kids Press
Camden, New York

The Adirondack Kids #3
The Lost Lighthouse

Justin & Gary VanRiper
Copyright © 2003. All rights reserved.

First Paperback Edition, February 2003

Cover illustration by Susan Loeffler
Illustrated by Glenn Guy
Illustration of Northern Goshawk feather by Justin VanRiper
Cover Design and Production by Nancy Did It!, Blossvale, NY

Benjamin Harrison photographs appear with permission
from President Benjamin Harrison Home, Indianapolis, Indiana.

Northern Goshawk photographs appear courtesy
of Jim Spencer & Dave Armstrong.
Portrait of Justin and Gary VanRiper
at Shoal Point Lighthouse by Carol VanRiper.

Published by
Adirondack Kids Press
39 Second Street
Camden, New York 13316

Printed in the United States of America
by Patterson Printing, Michigan

Library of Congress Cataloguing-in-Publication Data

CIP applied for

ISBN 0-9707044-2-9

The man was on the porch now,
staring at them as they slowly pulled away.

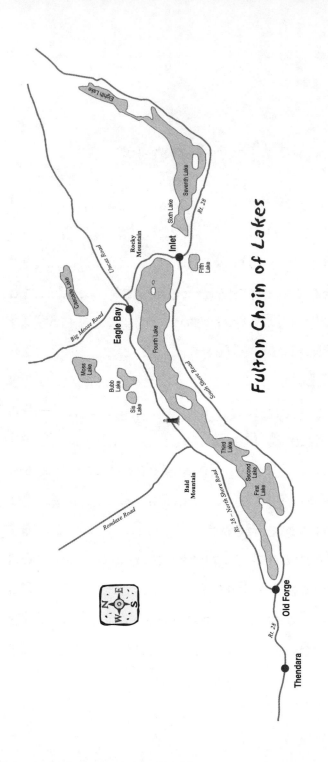

Fulton Chain of Lakes

Contents

For Nanny & Grandpa
thanks for camp!

chapter one

The Storm

"Get the worm yourself," Justin Robert said. "I'm trying to draw."

Nick Barnes sat in the middle seat of the putt-putt and leaned forward to plunge his fingers into the white pint-sized container filled with fat, moist night crawlers. The small aluminum boat rocked as he moved.

"Cut it out, Nick," said Justin, and frowned. He turned his # 2 pencil upside down and began erasing vigorously. "You made me mess up again."

A deep sigh came from the back of the boat. "Was I wrong? Didn't we come here to catch the biggest fish in the Fulton Chain?"

It was Jackie Salsberry, the only native Adirondack kid among the three best friends who spent every summer together on Fourth Lake in the Adirondack Mountains. They had been fishing for hours well off the west end of Algier Island. It was the coolest place to be during the extended hot and humid weather. She cast her line out toward the south shoreline.

"Yes," said Nick, happy to have Jackie on his side for a change. "I am going to catch the biggest fish in these waters and win the *Adirondack Kids Fishing Derby* this year, or my name isn't Captain Ahab!" He worked the wriggling worm onto his hook and threw his own line into deeper water out and away from Algier Island.

"Well, your name is *not* Captain Ahab," said Justin. "And you'll be lucky if you catch a cold."

Jackie pointed into the direction Nick had cast his line. "I thought you didn't use bobbers," she said.

"I usually don't," said Nick.

"That's not a bobber," said Justin, and laughed. "That's another one of those ping-pong balls Nick dropped into the lake last weekend. Look, there's another one – and another one."

Nick had won the chance to fly in the seaplane over Fern Park in Inlet for the annual ping-pong ball drop on the Fourth of July. But he pulled the release lever too soon after take-off, and hundreds of colorful balls cascaded from the bottom of the plane and into Fourth Lake.

"We'll fish them out of the lake before we leave this spot," said Jackie.

Nick hung his head. "How many does that make today?" he asked, glumly.

"Fourteen," said Justin, and changed the subject. "Hey, how does this look?" he asked, and smiled. The budding artist held his small sketch book open for Nick and Jackie to glance back at over their shoulders.

"It looks really great," said Nick. "Um, what exactly is it?"

Justin's smile disappeared. "It's Dax on the bow of the boat," said Justin, and pointed firmly with his pencil. "See, there's her head and legs and tail. And there's the Shoal Point Lighthouse in the background, right there."

"It really is pretty good," said Jackie. "Especially for just beginning."

Justin's calico cat jumped from the bow of the boat and landed right next to the minnow bucket. She peered into the pail and slowly lifted her paw.

"Don't even think about it, Dax," said Justin, and scooped her up and away from the bait. He noticed Jackie was squinting – staring hard, well beyond her bobber, toward the southern shoreline. She looked concerned. "What are you looking at?" he asked.

Jackie began reeling in her line quickly. "The Red Admirals are dancing," she said. "We had better get going right now."

Nick scanned the shoreline. "I don't hear any music," he said. "And I definitely don't see anyone dancing."

Jackie barked out a command. There was urgency in her voice. "Pull up the anchor, Justin," she said, as she reeled in the last of her line and dropped the pole into the boat. With a jerk on the engine cord, she had the small outboard motor running. "Red Admirals are butterflies," she said. "They dance in the air together at dusk, or when...."

3

She was interrupted by a sudden boom of thunder. "...or when it's going to *storm*."

4

chapter two

Something Fishy

The sudden thunder caught them all by surprise. Nick fell backward off his broad aluminum seat and nearly lost his grasp on his pole. "Oh, no you don't," he said, clutching his gear. He willed his body back into a seated position.

Justin nearly let the thick, slimy anchor rope slip through his hands. He couldn't see the butterflies Jackie was talking about, but he could feel some wings fluttering about inside his stomach. "Got it," he yelled, and the small metal weight banged inside the bow. He yanked his yellow rain slicker from underneath his own seat, pulled it on and slipped his pencil and sketch book into one of its wide inside pockets.

The small outboard engine buzzed as Jackie gripped the throttle and hit the gas.

At first the boat cut across the water surface with ease, but with the thunder came wind. And with wind, came waves. Big waves.

"I've never seen it like this before," yelled Jackie.

Dax jumped onto Justin's lap. He wrapped his

arm around his pet and held tightly to the side of the boat. As the pointed bow rose and fell into one giant wave after another, water splashed into his face. Justin had great confidence in Jackie, but he could not bring himself to utter a word. Even Nick was silent.

Jackie shouted over the noise of the engine and the thunder. Her long blond hair whipped in the wind. "Forget the island," she said. "I'm going for the south shore."

Justin grasped his white bucket hat and stuffed it onto the seat between his legs so it wouldn't blow away. He held Dax tighter and looked back over the low mountains. Dark and fast moving clouds swept in on them like a bird of prey as the sky changed color from gray to cobalt to green. There was lightning and another crack of thunder.

Nick screamed. "Can't we go faster?" he called. "Make it go faster."

"Here comes the rain," yelled Justin.

Another bolt of lightning flashed over them, and a few drops hit their skin followed almost immediately by a shower of pellets that pounded the passengers and pinged off the aluminum boat with the sound of rapid machine gun fire.

"Ouch," said Nick. "That stings."

"It's not rain," yelled Jackie. "It's hail."

The small icy balls began to accumulate at the bottom of the boat. It grew dark and they could all hear a roar behind them, but no one dared to look back. Jackie pressed through the last of the giant waves, maneuvered their craft into a small cove and crashed through some low hanging branches along the shore.

She beached the boat and slipping over the icy bottom, the three Adirondack kids jumped over the side and ran inland. They passed through dense vegetation in a frantic search for some kind of shelter.

Lightning flashed and acted like a giant strobe helping to light the way. Breathless, they came to the edge of a thick stand of pines that continued to heave and creak in the deafening wind. What appeared to be a narrow crooked building was located near dead center of a small clearing out in front of them. With heads down and arms raised to shield their eyes from the hail, they raced toward it. Unable to locate a door they finally entered the structure squeezing through a narrow crack in the wall.

Sheets of rain and things that sounded too big to be rain now battered the building, but insulated from the elements raging outside, the three Adirondack kids finally had a moment to consider what had happened to them.

Justin's mind was still in the boat, rocking in the waves, wondering if he would see the shore, even his parents, ever again. He was stirred alert by the sound of heavy breathing. His own. Then Nick's and Jackie's, which he also felt. As his eyes adjusted to the dim light provided by small open windows near the roof, he noticed they each had their backs

7

against an inside wall, but were still very near to each other. It was as if they were standing in a tall, narrow tube. The persistent flashes of lightning helped him make out the look of confusion and fear that waxed across the face of each of his friends. Dax crouched at the center of their intimate circle.

No one said anything for nearly ten minutes. But it seemed like hours.

The rain stopped and the wind subsided almost as suddenly as it had arrived. Small shafts of sunlight poured through the windows above, and actually penetrated small holes in the old walls all around them. Justin felt his body relax. He loosened his life jacket and his breathing returned to normal.

Slowly, the three friends exited their sanctuary.

"Listen," said Nick. "What's that slapping sound?"

As they tumbled out onto the damp earth, they rose to find a dozen small fish flopping all around them. "Where did these come from?" asked Justin.

"Don't just stand there," said Jackie. "Let's get them back into the water."

Dax smacked her lips.

"Look for a big one with a red tag," said Nick. "That's the one worth a million bucks."

Justin struggled to pick up even one fish. Just when he thought he had one secure, it twisted its slick body from side to side and slipped from his hands. "Don't you know I'm trying to save you?" he said, and bent over to try again.

After multiple trips with fish in hand, the rescue

8

squad had created a small herd path through the pines from the clearing to the cove. Exhausted, they finally turned their full attention to their own life-saving shelter.

It registered with Jackie first. "How in the world did *that* get here?" she said.

"This has got to be the strangest day of my whole life," said Nick.

Slightly tipped to one side,
the old lighthouse was anchored in place
by a tangle of roots and vines...

10

chapter three

Held Hostage

"A lighthouse?" said Justin. "A lighthouse in the middle of the woods?"

They were right. Well, half right. The old wooden structure was weather beaten and appeared to be severed with only the top portion sticking upright from the ground. Slightly tipped to one side, the building was anchored in place by a tangle of roots and vines all twisted about the outer shell. A few broken shingles littered the ground.

"It looks like the leaning tower of pizza," said Nick.

"That's Pisa," said Jackie, and sighed. "The leaning tower of Pisa."

"It looks a lot like the Shoal Point Lighthouse, but without the whole bottom half," Justin said. He looked in the direction of the lake and then back at the lighthouse. "But it's way too far in the woods to do boats any good."

"I vote we use it as a clubhouse," said Nick.

"We don't even know who owns this property," said Jackie. "Besides, it looks kind of creepy."

Kek-kek-kek-kek-kek-kek-kek-kek-kek-kek.

11

The piercing primeval scream from the woods sent shivers down each of their spines.

Nick suddenly fell hard to the ground, looked at Justin, and frowned. "Why did you shove me?" he asked.

"I didn't touch you," said Justin, and helped his friend to his feet. That's when he noticed a large gash in the back of Nick's life jacket.

Kek-kek-kek-kek-kek-kek-kek-kek-kek-kek.

"What's making that eerie sound?" asked Justin. He looked all around.

"What hit me?" asked Nick. "What hit me?"

"Let's get back into the lighthouse," commanded Jackie.

They bumped into each other trying to squeeze back through the narrow opening. Dax was already inside.

Nick reached over his back and groped to inspect the damage to his life jacket. His fingers fit easily inside three large gashes near the left shoulder area of the vest. "I'm in trouble now," he said. "This is brand new."

Justin was trying to peek through one of the small holes in the wall. "But what's out there?" he said. "I can't see anything. Someone will have to go up to get a look."

They peered up the lighthouse's nine foot shaft that narrowed like a candle as it rose. Only the silhouette of cobwebs stretched across their field of view and hung between them and the windows near the roof.

Jackie was not afraid of snakes, salamanders or almost anything you could find underneath an old rotting log. But there was one thing she couldn't take. Spiders. "I'll pass," she said.

"I'd better stay down here and protect Dax," Justin reasoned.

Nick groaned. "Sure," he said. "Make *me* do it."

"Well, your life jacket is already ruined," said Justin.

"Oh, so just let the creature tear it to pieces," said Nick. He gulped. "Or even me."

Jackie pointed to the sides of the walls. "Look, there are wooden beams every few feet all the way up," she said. "Just grab with your hands and use them like a ladder. We'll help you get started."

Nick hedged. "There hasn't been any screeching in a while. Maybe the Bigfoot is gone."

"Bigfoot?" said Justin. "Where did you come up with Bigfoot?"

"Come on, up you go," said Jackie, and gave Nick a gentle push to get him started on the ascent.

Nick looked down. "Can I at least use Justin's bucket hat to block the cobwebs?"

They pushed him upward again.

Nick closed his eyes and then spit as he felt the webbing brush across his face. "There's stuff hanging on the walls up here," he said.

"Like what?" Justin asked.

"I don't know," said Nick. "It looks like old tools and stuff." His elbow accidentally dislodged a flat object and it fell. "Look out below," he called, after it had hit the ground.

"Watch it," said Justin. "Don't go clobbering us with a hammer or something."

Nick slowly pulled himself upward, a beam at a time. As the structure narrowed toward the top, he could rest his back against the wall behind him and peer over the ledge of a window. He clutched the rotted sill and searched the ground below.

There was no movement. There was no sound. "I don't see anything at all," he said.

Jackie urged him on. "Well, there are windows all the way around the top up there. Look behind you."

"I can't," said Nick.

"Why not?" asked Justin.

"I'm stuck," said Nick. It was true. Nick was not a small boy. And with the life jacket on, he was wedged in the narrow opening. There was panic in his voice. "Help me," he said. "I mean it. Help me right now."

"Unbuckle your life jacket," suggested Justin.

Before Jackie could protest, Nick grunted, twisted his arm around in front of him, and unsnapped the buckle. His body was suddenly released and he fell onto his wide-eyed friends below. The lighthouse moaned as their combined weight slammed against a wall.

"This is ridiculous," said Jackie, as they untangled and struggled to stand up. "Let's just run for it before whatever it is out there comes in here after us, or steals our boat."

14

"Unless the storm washed the boat away," said Justin. That dreadful thought had just occurred to him.

The three hostages quickly squeezed back outside and made a dead run for the path. Pine boughs brushed their arms, thighs and ankles as they whisked through the trees. The boat was still there and they began to shove it back fully into the water. Then it hit Justin. *Dax*, he thought.

Jackie and Nick were preoccupied with starting the engine and getting back home. Neither of them noticed Justin run back into the woods.

chapter four

Kek-Kek-Kek-Kek-Kek

Justin hesitated at the edge of the clearing. "Come on, Dax," he whispered. He could see her face just inside the lighthouse. *What is she so afraid of?* he thought. He took a deep breath and bolted for the lighthouse, and then he knew.

Kek-kek-kek-kek-kek-kek-kek-kek. Justin turned to face his attacker and dropped to the ground just in time to avoid an aerial attack from a giant bird.

Kek-kek-kek-kek-kek-kek-kek-kek-kek-kek.... It screamed again as it passed over him with its massive wing span and landed high up in one of the tall standing pines.

Justin scrambled to his feet and ran for Dax. She pulled away from him. As he reached in to grab her he noticed a small book at her feet. *That must be what Nick knocked off the wall*, he thought. With Dax firmly under one arm and the book in his hand, he dashed back through the woods, faster than Nick would have run after his favorite sandwich.

"Come on, Justin, get in," called Jackie.

Justin needed no urging. He splashed through ankle deep water and Dax leaped from his arm making a graceful landing onto the front seat of the boat. Her savior lunged over the side and nearly tipped the boat over. He protected the book in his hand as he tumbled into the metal ribbed bottom and splashed into the shallow pool of icy water created by the melted hail. "Go, go, go," he said. "It's after me!"

"We know. We heard it," said Jackie. She hit the gas, turned the boat abruptly around, raced through the cove and sped back out into the open water of Fourth Lake.

The storm hadn't lasted long, but long enough for the temperature to drop a number of degrees. There was actually a slight chill in the air which was also crisp and clean and filled their lungs deeply.

Before Justin could explain what he had seen, they sat in awe as they moved along the shoreline and saw some of the damage the storm had done. Trees were down everywhere. Some were missing just their tops. Others were laying sideways with their roots sticking up into the air. Then there were stretches where everything looked totally normal.

There was only one other motor boat on the entire lake and it began to approach them near Gull Rock where Cedar Island came fully into view.

"It's Ranger Bill," said Justin, who had reassumed his position at the bow of the boat.

Ranger William S. Buck was the area's official Forest Ranger. He and his wife were also best friends with Jackie's parents. He maneuvered his craft alongside the putt-putt. "Are you kids all right?" he asked. His forehead bore wrinkles of deep concern.

Jackie smiled and gave him a thumbs up. "We're fine," she said. "We'll follow you."

The ranger nodded and motored ahead – the Adirondack kids enjoying the comfort of an official escort home.

Justin could see his parents waiting on the dock. Dax was usually the first one out of any boat, but not this time. With fishing gear already in hand, Justin leapt out of the putt-putt and glanced down the shoreline. Nick's parents were one dock down, also awaiting their son's safe return.

"You're next, Nick," said Jackie. "See you tomorrow, Justin." She waved as they sped away.

Justin's parents both bent over and embraced him at the same time. He couldn't remember ever being squeezed so hard.

"We were so worried about you," said his mom, during the impromptu family reunion. "The storm came in so quickly, it caught everyone by surprise."

Justin looked past his parents and toward the cabin. He blinked, and looked again. A huge pine tree had crashed into the roof. A corner of the upstairs sleeping porch was sheared completely off. More trees in the yard were down and branches were strewn everywhere. The entire scene looked surreal. "What happened to my room?" he asked. "What are we going to do?"

"The storm did some damage, but everything's going to be fine," his dad said, calmly. "We're just going to tarp the portion of the roof that's gone, and begin repairs on it tomorrow. We'll all camp out in the living room tonight – it'll be candles and lanterns and a good board game."

"I get to pick the game," said Justin, and smiled. His dad always seemed to know exactly how to make him feel totally safe and secure.

There was a lot to look at behind
the counter at the Tamarack Cafe.

chapter five

Diner Conversation

The next morning there were several quick and unanimous votes during an official meeting at Pioneer Village. Wind had not only damaged Justin's and Nick's family cabins. It had also devastated the small community of stick homes and shoppes the three friends built every year that was located in the woods between the two family's camps.

They had decided to keep the lighthouse a secret, for now.

Justin described the giant bird that had swooped down on him as best as he could. He even tried to draw a picture of it for them in his sketch book. Jackie and Nick both doubted the size of the bird he described, but Jackie promised to look it up later in one of her field guides.

And instead of village clean-up and reconstruction, they voted for breakfast at the Tamarack, a decision influenced earlier with encouragement from Justin's mom and dad. "They want me out of the way while they're fixing the roof," explained Justin.

"That's great," said Nick. "The power's still out at

our place, and we couldn't cook, anyway."

"The Tamarack does have power," said Jackie.

"And hot pancakes and eggs and bacon," said Nick, who knew the entire menu by heart. It was their favorite place to eat together and had become a summer tradition for them.

"So, let's go," said Justin.

"The putt-putt or the bikes?" asked Jackie.

Justin jumped to his feet. "I vote we use our wheels," he said.

Nick wanted to know which mode of transportation would be quicker, but Justin and Jackie were already running to the boathouse to grab their bicycles.

The Tamarack Cafe in the center of Inlet was always busy, but this particular morning, it was jam packed.

As Justin, Jackie and Nick parked their bikes on the sidewalk they learned power was still out in a great number of the outlying homes, camps and cottages and it seemed everyone had a storm story to tell.

Most folks waiting in line wanted a table. The three Adirondack kids moved just inside the squeaky screen door and jumped on three empty stools at the counter.

"The regular, you guys?" asked the waitress, and smiled.

"Yes, please," said Justin.

Jackie and Nick nodded.

There was a familiar voice coming from the stool located at the end of the counter near the large front plate glass window. Old Mr. Scott sat in the same spot every morning sipping on black coffee, and reading a book. He had his swivel seat spun around and was in the middle of addressing everyone in the entire cafe. "I lived through the Great Blowdown in 1950," he said. "I'm telling you once and for all – this was no straight line wind. No, sir. The way the trees were all twisted around – and the damage done just here and there – it was a tornado touched down for sure."

Someone challenged him from a nearby table. "Sorry, mister. There are no tornadoes in the Adirondacks."

"That's where you are wrong, sonny," Mr. Scott said. "1845. That's right. Midway through the 19th century, a tornado was recorded in the region."

"I don't know if the old man's right or not," said a tourist sitting next to Justin at the counter. "All I know is that the wind blew over a monster tree at the place we were staying on the lake. The roots from the tree shot up through the ground and half a boat house was sent flying through the air like a missile."

A woman called out from a booth in the back of the establishment. "I read that a twister once touched down and picked up a pond full of frogs and dropped them all a half mile away," she said. "Anybody see it rain frogs yesterday?"

Everyone laughed.

Mr. Scott grunted. "It was a tornado," he said, and turned to finish his coffee.

As the public chatter returned to private conversations, Justin turned to Jackie. "I wonder if that's how that lighthouse got so deep into the woods," he said.

"And those fish flopping all over the ground in the middle of the storm," said Jackie. "That might explain how they got there."

Justin finished his orange juice. "I wonder if that book we found has any clues about the lighthouse," he said.

"What's in the book?" asked Jackie.

"I don't even know yet," said Justin. "The cover looks really old." Then his eyes grew wide. "Oh, no. I left it in my sleeping bag in the family room. I hope Mom didn't find it."

Nick had ignored all the talking that swirled around him, and had simply concentrated on devouring his pancakes, eggs and bacon. There was a lot to look at on the wall behind the counter – old Adirondack signs and banners, a poster of Smokey the Bear and a license plate that read, LUV2FISH. But it was the mounted Tiger Muskie hanging directly in front of him with its long, wide body and gaping mouth lined with sharp teeth he couldn't take his eyes from. "I need to catch one just like that," he finally said. "Or one like this, or like this." He pointed to photographs that were printed all over the cafe's menu of local people holding their trophy trout and pike. "But mine needs a big red contest tag on its fin."

Jackie dropped their breakfast money onto the counter. "Let's go get that book," she said.

Justin popped the last bit of toast into his mouth, glanced up at the trophy fish on the wall, then over at Nick. "Dream on the way back to camp, Captain Ahab," he said, and grabbed him by the arm. They were on the road, peddling up Route 28 back to Eagle Bay before the squeaky screen door of the cafe banged shut.

chapter six

Sketchy Clues

Justin returned home to find several men hammering on the roof. The large tree that had done the damage to the sleeping porch was already sawn into pieces and was laying in small sections right where it had finally dropped on the ground. His mom and dad were gathering and stacking small broken branches that were littered about the yard.

"Just in time to help," said his mom, and handed him a pair of gray work gloves.

After pitching in with an hour of late morning labor, he dashed into the house and ransacked his sleeping bag that was still stashed behind the couch. The small book with a brown leather cover was still there. He sighed with relief, and then ran out to the boathouse to meet Jackie and Nick who were already there waiting for him.

"It's no use trying to meet in Pioneer Village with all that mess," said Nick. "One good thing is that we'll have enough new sticks to build a whole city."

"I brought my field guide so we can look for the giant bird you saw," said Jackie. "But you go first.

What's inside the old book?"

Justin sat down in a tube on the boathouse floor and slowly opened the front cover. He carefully turned the loose brittle pages. There was only one small drawing and some writing, most of which was unintelligible. "It's a journal," he said. "But whoever owned it didn't write very much."

"Do you mean it's like a diary?" asked Nick. He jumped into the Robert's motorboat docked in the slip. "Read it out loud. Maybe there's some secret stuff in it."

Jackie agreed. She unfolded a lawn chair and sat down holding the field guide on her lap.

"The writing is kind of funny," said Justin. "Okay, here's something." He cleared his throat to read.

"Went for lake trout with P.B.H. Not just a great shot with his double barrel, he can fish too."

"What is P.B.H.?" asked Nick.

"I have no idea," said Justin. "Here's another one."

"August 19 and frogs from the pond again for breakfast with P.B.H. and the ladies."

"Frogs?" asked Nick. "They ate *frogs* for breakfast? That's sick."

Justin flipped gently back through the pages. "It says P.B.H. and Ex P.B.H. and B.H. a lot in here."

27

"You'd think eating frogs would give you warts on your lips," said Nick.

Jackie moved her chair and looked over Justin's shoulder. "Wait, go back to that one drawing," she said and squinted to focus her vision. "It's a man in a guide boat, with a fancy hat on. And look at that beard."

Nick grabbed a rope suspended from the ceiling and pulled himself out of the boat and back up onto the wooden floor. "Let me see," he said. "He's not chowing down on a frog is he?" He leaned down over Justin's other shoulder. "Hey, it looks like he's wearing one of your bucket hats, but with the brim turned up all the way around." He looked again. "Either that, or he draws a lot worse than you."

Jackie corrected him. "He or *she*," she said. "And that's not a bucket hat, it's a derby." She leaned back in her chair. "This book must be pretty old. Maybe someone at the historical society in Old Forge can tell us more about it."

"Maybe," said Justin. "There is a name under the drawing. It looks like... 'I. Chuck'."

Nick shook his head. "I, Tarzan," he said, and swinging again on the rope landed back into the boat. "That person sure had bad English."

Justin closed the book and turned to Jackie. "Okay, look in your field guide for a giant gray bird," he said. "And I mean giant with a capital G."

Jackie flipped to the index, then quickly to a painting toward the front of the book. "How about this one?" she said, and held up the guide.

"That's it!" Justin said, startling both of his friends. "There must be a hundred birds in that book. How did you get it on the first try?"

"You said capital G, so that's where I looked," Jackie said. "This is a Northern Goshawk, with a capital G."

"So, how big is a goshawk?" asked Nick. "Is it bigger than a hummingbird?"

Justin frowned. "Oh, that was so funny I forgot to laugh," he said.

"Whoa – this *is* big," said Jackie. "It says here the Northern Goshawk is two feet tall with a wing span of 45 inches." She slowly moved her finger down the page. "And listen to this – it says the goshawk is bold and aggressive and that when it has young birds it will attack human intruders who come near the nest, relentlessly."

"What does *relentlessly* mean?" asked Nick.

"It means like you going after a Tiger Muskie with a red tag on its tail that's worth a million dollars," said Justin. "Or like you talking about frogs and warts," he continued. "It means you just never, ever give up." He worked himself up out of the tube and walked over to a bench at the rear of the boathouse. "I'll show you how big that bird was. Let's figure out 45 inches."

Taking a loose piece of ski rope, Justin ran it across the top of a steel tackle box that had a one foot raised ruler stamped onto it. He marked off 45 inches of rope, 12 inches at a time. Then he handed the rope to Jackie and spread his arms like wings. "Measure me" he said. "See which is bigger, me or the goshawk."

"Well, you're definitely taller," said Nick.

As Jackie began to stretch the rope across the length of Justin's extended arms, he began flapping them up and down. "Stop it, Justin," she said. "Hold still."

"I can't help it, I'm a goshawk," Justin said. Jackie glared at him. "Now you look just like the bird that dove at me," he said, and laughed. But he did hold his arms still.

"It's almost a perfect match," said Jackie. "Your arms going across like that are almost exactly the same length as the goshawk's entire wing span."

Justin ran straight at Nick with wide eyes, flapping his arms. "Kek-kek-kek-kek," he yelled, trying to imitate the bird.

His mother walked in on the mock attack, and shook her head. "Excuse me," she said. "Justin, I'm headed to Old Forge for two new porch screens. Stay nearby."

"Let us go with you, Mom," Justin said. "We need to stop at the history building."

His mom protested. "I'm not going to be long," she said.

"We don't need long, Mom," he said. "Really."

"It may not even be open after that storm," she said.

"Please?" he said.

"Measure me," Justin said.
"See which is bigger, me or the goshawk."

She put her hands on her hips.
"Pleeeeease?"

chapter seven

P.B.H.

Justin sat in the front seat of the jeep and turned the radio on. News of the storm and all the damage it had done still dominated the airwaves.

The station was conducting a live interview with members of a family who had been trapped in the woods at a campsite.

"Turn it up so I can hear it," said Nick from the back seat.

Justin leaned forward and adjusted the volume.

"We tried to tie down our tent and it just blew away," said a young voice on the radio. "Trees were dropping around us everywhere, and the thunder and lightning were unbelievable."

The station cut to an advertisement.

"That was just like what happened to us," said Justin.

It was normally only fifteen minutes from Eagle Bay to Old Forge. But this trip was not normal. The storm had uprooted trees all along Route 28, and the trees had ripped down phone lines. Lights flashed on huge trucks parked roadside and workers with chain saws were everywhere. Weaving through the obstacle course directed by men in orange vests waving orange flags, they finally entered the village.

"Just a few minutes, I mean it," said Mrs. Robert as she dropped the three researchers off at the historical society on Main Street. They quickly ran up the wood steps and onto the porch of the stately home that was converted into a museum. The atmosphere created by the rich collection of area books, maps and artifacts contained inside commanded respect and they stopped running as they entered the front door, without even being told.

"Yes, it's open," said Justin. He whispered to Nick. "I'll ask about the book, but remember – the lighthouse is a secret."

Nick looked annoyed. "I know," he said, and then noticed Jackie looking at him. "I know – I *know*."

A tall, thin woman in a white blouse and blue jeans greeted them with a wide smile, just inside the lobby. A hefty man thumbing through a stack of papers was seated at a large black table in the center of an adjoining room. "Can I help you?" the tall woman asked, and pushed back her long, dark hair. "My name is Miss Holmes."

"Yes," said Justin. He handed the historian the leather book. "We found this and wondered if you could tell us anything about it."

She reached for the glasses that rested on the top of her head and cradling the book gently in her hands, slowly began to turn the pages.

Justin could tell by the way she was holding the

book it had great value – it was the same way he held his favorite trading cards. "We noticed whoever wrote it kept saying P.B.H. and B.H.," he said.

Nick yawned. "I think I've figured out what it means," he said. "Pretty Boring History."

"Oh my," said Miss Holmes.

The tone in her voice captured the full attention of all three Adirondack kids. Even the man at the big black table turned around to listen. There was a long, silent pause and then – "I am quite certain P.B.H. stands for President Benjamin Harrison," she said. "Yes, I am certain of it."

"President of what?" asked Nick. "The Moose Club?"

Jackie gently pushed his shoulder." No, you goof," she said. "President of the United States." She looked at the historian. "He was the one with the big house on Second Lake, right?"

Miss Holmes nodded. "Absolutely correct," she said. "President Harrison was the 23rd President of the United States. He loved the Adirondacks and built a camp on Second Lake in 1896 called the Berkeley Lodge."

Nick looked puzzled. "But it says in that book that B.H. fished and hunted and ate frogs," he said. "I thought all presidents did was work and give speeches and other boring stuff like that."

Miss Holmes removed her glasses. "Would you mind if I made photo copies of these pages?" she asked. "And could you jot your name, address and phone number in the guest book for me?"

"Sure," said Justin.

The copier was in a back room. It was old and loud.

"May I ask where you found this journal?" Miss Holmes called over the noise of the machine. "It is an incredible find."

"We definitely didn't find it near any old lighthouse," yelled Nick.

Justin and Jackie looked at him in disbelief.

"Oh," said the historian, as she reentered the room and handed Justin the book. "That's too bad. It would make sense with the reference the writer makes to a lighthouse."

Justin looked surprised. "We didn't notice anything about a lighthouse when we read through it," he said. "But some of the words and sentences were hard to make out."

Nick interrupted. "Well, nobody would want to go to the beat up building where we found that old book anyway," he said. "Especially not with a giant gray bird with razor sharp claws waiting to swoop down on anybody that gets near the place."

Justin noticed the large man at the big black table turn his chair fully around to face them. It made him feel uneasy. He slid the book under his arm and slightly turned his body to keep it from sight.

The front door of the museum swung open and Mrs. Robert walked in. "Come along Justin," she said. "We have to go now."

Nick was the first one out the door, across the

sidewalk and into the jeep. Jackie piled in behind him.

Justin jumped into the front seat, and turned to roll down the window as his mom entered the driver's side. He changed his mind, and let go of the handle. The man who was sitting at the big black table was on the porch now, staring at them as they slowly pulled away.

chapter eight

Moby Dick

The next morning the three Adirondack kids were already back to their favorite haunt near Algier Island, where Jackie was sure a trophy fish lurked in the Fourth Lake waters below. Dax was curled up and asleep on an extra life jacket at the bow of the putt-putt.

"Why didn't you just draw the guy a map?" asked Justin, as he baited his hook. He pointed his pole at the Shoal Point Lighthouse situated behind them on the north shore of the lake. "There's only one light-house in almost the whole Adirondack Park and you have to say to the lady, 'well, we didn't find the book anywhere near a lighthouse.'"

Nick already had his line in the water. "That was to throw her off," he said.

"Didn't you see that guy watching us?" said Justin. "He listened to us talk about the book. He knows how valuable it is. That's why he followed us right out the front door of the building."

Jackie cast her bait again toward the edge of the reeds along the south shoreline. "We have two days left to win this fishing contest," she said. "I suggest we concentrate right now on pike and muskies." She paused. "You know that book isn't even really ours," she said, thoughtfully. "We don't even know who owns the property we were on."

Justin didn't say anything, but he knew she was right.

"Whoa, I've got a bite – I've got a bite," said Nick. His pole was bent over in the shape of a rainbow. "Look at my pole," he said, excitedly. "It's Moby Dick!"

Justin could feel his own heart thumping, but he noticed Jackie seemed to be ignoring the whole ordeal. "Come on Captain Ahab," he said. "Reel him in."

Nick was sweating. "I'm trying to," he said. "It's really fighting hard." He reeled in his line a little more. "Get the net ready."

Justin set down his pole and grabbed the net, ready to lean over the side of the putt-putt and scoop out the scaly beast.

Nick reeled in a little more line and there was a splash at the surface of the dark water alongside the boat. "Grab it," said Nick. "Is there a red tag on it? Don't let it get away."

Justin couldn't tell what kind of fish it was. He reached out and under the golden flash that was struggling on the end of his friend's line. He sat back on his seat and pulled the creature from the net's tangle of soft, black webbing.

"That's it?" said Nick. "A little sunny?"

Justin looked amused, and held up the tiny fish dangling at the end of Nick's line. "Moby Dick is Moby Dinky," he said.

Jackie turned to see the wee fish at the end of Nick's line and tried not to laugh. But she couldn't help it. "Nick, please pass me the bait," she said. "Oh, I'm sorry, that's your trophy fish." She began laughing uncontrollably.

"You definitely need this one mounted," said Justin as he carefully removed the hook from the fish's tiny mouth. "Maybe they'll put it on the wall at the Tamarack Cafe."

Jackie agreed. "I am sure they will," she said. "They'll put it right inside the Tiger Muskie's mouth."

Dax lifted her head and opened her eyes. Even she looked at the fish and yawned.

That made Nick laugh, and soon the sound of all three cheerful voices echoed as one across the lake.

Justin reached over the side of the boat to let the sunfish go. As its small thin body slipped from his hand and slowly swam from view, a glint of light from the island caught his attention. There was someone on the shore with a pair of binoculars looking in their direction. Justin's smile disappeared. "Start the motor, Jackie," he said, and stood to pull up the anchor. "Start it now."

chapter nine

Hide & Peek

Nick looked up at the sky. "Are the butterflies dancing again – is there another storm coming?"

"No, worse," said Justin. He pointed toward Algier Island. "It's that weird guy from the muscum. The man that followed us out the door. He's on the island and he is watching us."

"Do you mean the man over there getting into that huge boat?" asked Jackie.

Justin dropped the anchor into the boat, shook the lake water from his hands and sat down. "Yes," he said. "Head back around the island and we'll lose him."

Jackie revved the enginc and moved the putt-putt out of the man's view and quickly across the western shore of the island.

"His boat is bigger than ours," said Justin, as they made the turn and headed east toward home. "He's going to catch up to us fast."

"We have to find a place to hide," said Jackie, and moved the putt-putt closer along the edge of the island. They passed a few docks and Justin looked back at her. "Too open," she said. "He'll see the

41

boat and follow us ashore."

Then came a long stretch, wild with thick ever-green branches hanging low and out over the water. "Go in there," said Justin, and pointed to a mass of branches accessible by a dark, narrow opening.

Jackie angled the bow of the boat toward the spot and cut the engine. The small craft coasted into the bushy green cave and softly bumped against the rocky shore. "Grab hold of the branches above our heads so we don't slam against the rocks," she said.

"So where is he?" Nick said. "I don't hear anyone coming."

Justin scolded him. "Be quiet," he said. "That guy wouldn't even have known where we were if you had just kept quiet at the museum."

Nick frowned. "I'm tired of you always blaming me for everything that goes wrong," he said. "I'll bet that wasn't even the same guy. He probably wasn't even looking at us."

"Shhhhh." It was Jackie. She moved her finger from her lips and pointed to the lake.

The three sat silently and peered through the branches of their hideout. The large man's huge boat passed directly in front of them. The engine crackled, and made a low hum as it moved slowly forward. Poised behind the steering wheel, their pursuer systematically looked right – then left – then right – then left.

There was a shrill scrape, like the sound of a sword against a blackboard, that was followed immediately by a loud bang. The clatter came from the front of the putt-putt. Horrified, the Adirondack kids looked quickly for the source of the noise.

It was Dax. She had jumped onto the front seat next to Justin and sent a fishing pole sliding across the inside hull of the boat and then crashing to the aluminum floor. She loved the attention, and purred.

They quickly looked back toward the water. The man was no longer looking right and left. He was concentrating fully in their direction.

Everyone had their own way of dealing with the threat before them. Jackie quietly leaned over in case she needed to start the putt-putt. Nick looked back over his shoulder to see how hard it might be to scramble up and escape onto the island. Justin closed his eyes. *Please go away – please go away*, he thought.

An engine thundered, and Justin reopened his eyes. Water bubbled up from behind the man's huge boat and in a flash, it was gone.

The three friends let go of the branches and relaxed in their seats. Justin scooped up Dax and held her closely. "You almost gave us away," he said. Picking her up and gently scolding her was only an excuse in front of his companions to give her a hug.

"I don't understand," said Jackie. "Seeing him up close, that man didn't look mean at all. He was actually smiling."

Nick was on Justin's side now. "Sure he was smiling," he said. "When a bad guy is about to pounce on someone he's after, you don't think he'd be crying do you? That guy thought he had us, and he was happy about it." He looked at Justin. "It's too bad you're not a little better at drawing. You could have sketched a picture of his face for the police."

Jackie leaned back again and pulled the cord to start the putt-putt. It sputtered and stopped.

Justin was in deep thought and hadn't even heard Nick. "Why does that man want us?" he said, and thought some more. His eyes brightened. "I've got it. We know he wants the book. Maybe he thinks we know about other old things that are valuable too, like antique stuff."

"You mean like those tools on the lighthouse wall," Nick said.

Justin nodded.

Jackie pulled the cord on the engine again. And again, it sputtered and stopped.

"I don't know why old people like old stuff so much," said Nick. "I think it's pretty funny."

"Well, this isn't funny," said Jackie.

"What's wrong?" asked Justin. "Let's get going before that man circles the island and comes back. I want to go home."

"Me too," said Nick.

"Well then, grab the oars," Jackie said, and sighed. "We're out of gas."

chapter ten

Row, Row, Row Your Boat

Justin struggled to place the heavy, wooden oars into the oar locks, one at a time. Nick and Jackie assisted him. "Hold the end steady so I can slide the pin in," he said. The long, unruly paddles slapped the water, then banged against the hull. With a lot of effort, each oar finally slammed into place.

Then the real work began.

There was very little progress to show for all the waving, squeaking and splashing of the oars. It took nearly ten minutes stroke by painstaking stroke to move the boat from underneath their cover and out into open water. The Shoal Point Lighthouse was directly behind them, and with the loss of the engine, home ahead seemed a world away.

Justin groaned. "I hope that man has given up," he said. "My arms are killing me."

Nick sat slumped forward with his chin resting in his hands. "You just started," he said. He watched a dragonfly speed by. "Are we even moving?"

45

There was very little progress
to show for all the waving, squeaking
and banging of the oars.

Justin stopped to catch his breath. "Then you row," he said. "I can't even get both oars into the water at the same time."

Nick could tell how upset Justin was by his tone of voice. He didn't push it.

"Oh no," said Jackie. "This is not good."

"What?" asked Nick.

"I hear it," said Justin. "It's a boat. A really big boat."

Jackie jumped into the seat beside him. "Let's each take an oar," she said.

"Good idea," said Nick. "You can row like the Vikings."

The sound of the boat grew louder.

"Maybe we can make it back to the shore and hide again," said Justin. "Row!"

It was useless. They were caught in the middle of the channel – dead in the water.

"We're goners," said Nick.

Looks of terror slowly turned to joy as the bow of the loud boat finally appeared at the end of Algier Island. It was their good friend, Captain Conall McBride, making his tour of Fourth Lake delivering letters, postcards and packages on his mail boat, *Miss America*.

The three friends waved their arms frantically and cried out for help.

"Hello," called the captain, as he moved the mail boat alongside the putt-putt. At forty-five feet long, it dwarfed the small, stranded vessel. He looked down at them from the cabin window. "It looks like you can use some assistance. Am I right?"

"We're out of gas," called Justin. "Can you tow us to Eagle Bay?"

The captain smiled broadly through his snow white beard. "Of course I can," he said. "Take hold of this rope and tie it to your bow."

Jackie caught the nylon life line and looped it through the opening provided for the anchor at the front of the boat.

"Justin, why don't you come aboard and be my spotter," the captain said. He hooked a small ladder on the side of the mail boat. "You can keep an eye on your friends while I keep *Miss America* on course."

Justin scooped up Dax and climbed aboard the mail boat.

The captain was sitting at the wheel, and sneezed. "Oh, you've brought Dax with you," he said, and laughed. He knew without even turning around.

"I'm sorry you were allergic to her and had to give her away," Justin said. "But I'm glad, because she's been the best pet, ever."

The captain smiled. "Well, I knew you would give her a good home," he said. "And if I recall, it was she that adopted you!"

Justin looked out the back of the cab to check the putt-putt. Jackie and Nick were seated at each end of the boat across from each other. It looked like they were arguing about something. Justin sighed.

"So, what brings you to this end of Fourth Lake?" asked the captain.

"The fishing contest," said Justin. "Jackie said that it's the best place to catch the biggest fish."

The captain sneezed. "I see," he said. "Well, you'll have to go some to beat the fish the young lady caught by Cedar Island early this morning."

Justin looked anxious. "Did it have the red tag?" he asked.

The captain laughed. "No, no," he said. "But at 30 inches and 25 pounds, it'll be hard to beat for the largest fish."

Justin was relieved, and looked back to check the putt-putt again. The Shoal Point Lighthouse, becoming much smaller on the horizon as they moved steadily away, caught his attention. "You know a lot about the Fulton Chain, captain," he said. "Has there ever been another lighthouse on the lake?"

"That's a good question," said the captain. "Local legend has it there was another lighthouse on the Chain at one time. Sixteen feet high and maybe built by a camper. But no one knows for sure. It's a mystery. There are no pictures of it and no evidence has ever been found to prove it ever really existed."

Justin became excited. "How long ago do they think it was?"

"At least one hundred years," the captain said. He looked at Justin. "I don't know that many young people who are so interested in history. Why so many questions about the lighthouse?"

"I guess I'm just naturally curious," Justin said. He had learned over the course of his long ten years that one of the best ways to distract adults was to change the subject. "I can't believe we're at Gull Rock already." He pointed to a bird perched on a large green buoy that was bobbing near the pointed stone landmark. "Is that a Herring Gull, or a Ring-billed?"

"My eyes are not what they used to be," the captain said, and grabbed his binoculars. "Well, there is no black ring around the tip of its bill. It is definitely a Herring Gull."

Cedar Island loomed ahead. Captain McBride slowly turned the wheel to enter the bay and headed toward the marina. "I'll get you close," he said, and sneezed. "But you'll have to row through the docks to fill your tank with gas."

Justin nodded, but he was hardly paying attention. *One hundred years old?* he thought. *Wait until I tell Jackie and Nick. We've found the lost lighthouse!*

chapter eleven

Not Again

The early morning sun made the deep blue water on Fourth Lake sparkle. It was the first day of the new weekend and boats were everywhere. So were smiling faces. Except on the Robert's dock.

"Big deal," said Nick. He sat on the front edge of the dock with his legs crossed. The line at the end of his pole dropped in the water straight down in front of him. "So we found an old lighthouse with a bunch of old junk in it. Even if it's valuable stuff, we can't get near it because you said a monster bird is guarding it."

Jackie was really annoyed. No, she was more than annoyed. She was mad, and refused to cast her line again. "I don't even care about the lighthouse," she said, and stood gazing out onto the lake. "This is the last day of the fishing contest, and we are going to miss it because of some guy who is supposedly after us."

Justin was sitting on an Adirondack chair in the shade of the boathouse. He caught their drift. "You don't have to believe me about the goshawk or the thief," he said, defensively. He looked down at Nick. "How do you explain that awful scream in the woods and the rip in your life jacket?" He looked up at Jackie. "Why did that guy look at us with binoculars and then follow us in the channel?" He kicked the bucket that sat between them filled with tiny sunfish and rock bass they had caught all morning. Water sloshed over the open top and soaked the weathered wooden dock boards. "I'll tell you what. We'll just go back and one of you can catch Moby Dick. And then we can go to the new clubhouse in the woods and make a campfire and cook him. How about that?"

"And then we can have 'smores, right?" said Nick. He closed his eyes and began to rub his stomach. "I can taste them now. A beautiful sandwich of chocolate and melted marshmallows pressed between two crunchy graham cracker squares..."

Jackie slapped his arm and shook her head. "He's not serious, Nick," she said.

Nick looked disappointed.

"Let's be sensible about this," said Jackie. "We can go back and try fishing one more time. It's the weekend and people are everywhere. Even if that man is still there – and I doubt he is – he wouldn't dare try anything."

"Come on, Justin," said Nick, and stood to his feet. "I'm tired of catching these minnows from under the dock. He pointed to a small rock bass in the pail. "I've caught that one three times this morning already."

Jackie agreed. "I want to win this contest," she said. "Let's just go for it."

Nick dumped the pail of small fish back into the lake. "Come on, Justin," he said. "If we catch that one fish with a red tag, we'll be *gillionaires*."

Justin looked up into their pleading faces. "Well, maybe..." he said.

Jackie jumped on it. "That's a maybe..."

"I know, I know," said Justin, and sighed. "And a maybe is, 'yes'."

The putt-putt wasn't the fastest moving boat, even in smooth water. And once the three Adirondack kids had made the commitment to fish Jackie's favorite spot one more time before the fishing contest was over, the boat seemed to move even slower.

"Hey, look," said Nick. He pointed toward the north shore. "There's a dog swimming after mallards."

Jackie and Nick and even Dax watched the comical chase. Each time the dog would paddle up close to the birds, they would flap their wings exploding forward with a sudden burst in the water, and then come to rest again a few yards away just out of the panting canine's reach.

Justin wasn't going to be distracted. He ignored his friends and kept watch straight ahead. They were beyond Gull Rock and as far as he was concerned, they were moving back into enemy territory. He knew if the man closed in on them, they didn't have wings like the mallards to carry them away to safety.

Nick shrugged. "Well, I'm getting my pole ready now," he said.

"My arm is getting tired," said Jackie. She called on Justin. "Can you steer for a while?"

"Sure," Justin said. He knew she almost never gave up control – of anything. He was surprised at her offer, but didn't ask questions. Jackie slowed the boat down and the two quickly switched places.

Steering the putt-putt was fun, but he understood how it could get tiring. The vibration from the engine moved from his hand and through his whole arm. What was really odd was having to steer in the opposite direction you wanted the boat to go. Steer left to turn right. Steer right to turn left. It took some getting used to. He really liked driving the putt-putt and was disappointed as they approached their destination. They motored past the open picnic area at the eastern tip of Algier Island and into the channel along the southern shoreline.

Jackie raised her hand and barked a command. "Stop," she said.

Justin immediately cut the engine.

"There," she said, and pointed. "Look near the reeds."

It wasn't hard to see it. The body of a long fish moved effortlessly through the grassy green stalks. Its long narrow head and dorsal fin slightly broke through the surface of the shallow water.

"Muskie," said Jackie.

"There's two of them," said Justin.

Jackie shook her head. "No," she said. "Muskies usually travel alone. The front part sticking out of the water is its head. That thing sticking out behind it, is a fin near its tail."

Justin shifted in his seat, uneasily. Seeing a mammoth fish tacked up on the wall at the Tamarack Cafe was one thing. But seeing the fish alive and moving in the lake was quite different. "Muskies have a lot of teeth, don't they?" he asked.

"Oh, yes," said Jackie. "They have a bunch of them." She looked at Nick. "It's Moby Dick, captain. Are you ready?"

Nick smiled, weakly. "I'm not sure my line is strong enough," he said.

"It's plenty strong," Jackie said. "That's why I put that long steel leader on the end of your line. Use a minnow – the biggest one you can find." She cast her line toward the reeds. The live bait hit the water and the fish hit the bait. The tip of her pole bent straight over and touched the lake.

"No fair," said Nick.

Jackie howled. Dax sat right up. The tips of her ears went crazy at the sound.

Justin knew Jackie was aggressive, but he wasn't sure he had ever heard anyone make that noise before. At least it wasn't a yell of fear – it was of excitement.

"I can't believe it hit the bait that quick," Jackie said.

"Reel it in," Nick said. "Why aren't you reeling it in?"

Jackie waited and waited and then gripping the

pole with both hands tightly, pulled back hard. She howled again. "You're hooked good now," she said, and stood up to work the line. "Now you are *mine*."

Nick shrank back to give her more room. "I don't know which is scarier," he said. "You or the muskie."

Justin suddenly yanked the cord of the putt-putt and started the engine.

Jackie couldn't believe it. "No," she said. "What are you doing?"

Justin didn't reply. He gunned the engine and the boat lurched forward.

Jackie fell backward over her seat and her fishing line snapped. Then she snapped. "Justin Robert," she said, sternly. "Stop my boat right now."

"I can't," he said, and actually picked up speed.

"Why not?" she asked, and looked back over her shoulder. "Oh, no – not again."

chapter twelve

Bubble Head

The motor boat with the large man was moving slowly along the channel straight toward them.

"I don't think he's spotted us yet," said Nick. "Why don't you turn around?"

"There's no way we can out run him," said Justin. "Trust me. I have an idea."

As the putt-putt and the large motor boat passed by each other, Nick waved. Justin and Jackie glared at him. "I'm sorry you guys," he said. "I have no idea why I just did that."

The large man glanced over and slowly turned his boat around in a wide half circle to pursue the putt-putt.

Justin leaned forward in his seat as if a more aggressive position would somehow make their boat move faster.

The large boat closed in on them.

"Okay, Justin," said Jackie. "I believe you. There's a guy definitely after us. You can start your plan any time now."

Justin steered hard to his right and the small silver craft swerved into the cove – the same cove they had entered earlier to escape the violent summer storm. As they moved through the reeds nearer to the shore, the large motor boat behind them made another wide turn and cautiously entered the shallow water.

Justin stopped the engine and the putt-putt inched its way toward the low hanging branches that hid the entrance to their secret spot. "Move the branches," he said. "We're going in."

Jackie reached up from the bow of the boat to push up two low hanging limbs that guarded the opening.

There was an explosion of wings and water next to them and Jackie nearly fell into the lake. All three of the Adirondack kids screamed as a Great Blue Heron launched into the air right next to them. As if in slow motion, the four foot bird lifted off, the tip of its right wing brushing against the hull of the boat. The legs of a small frog protruded from the bird's long, narrow beak.

Jackie regained her composure, and reached out for the tree limbs again. The three friends ducked, using the thick branches as leverage to ease the boat under and through.

There was still a large scrape in the sandy shore where they had beached the boat several days earlier. This time they jumped out of the vessel and tugged it ashore. They listened and could still hear the low hum of the large motor boat lurking somewhere out in the cove.

"Let's go," said Justin, and reached into the boat to grab Dax.

"Go where?" Jackie asked.

"To the lighthouse," said Justin. Dax moved away from him.

"That's your plan," Jackie said. "Run and hide in the lighthouse?"

Nick shook his head. "But what about the giant goshawk?" he asked.

"What goshawk," said Justin. "There isn't any goshawk, remember? It's all in my imagination." He looked at Jackie. "And there's no man chasing us, either." He covered Dax up with an extra life jacket as she crouched on the floor of the boat. Her big green eyes stared up at him. "She knows," he said.

"Hey, I don't hear the motor boat anymore," said Nick. "Maybe he's gone."

"I hope he's wading ashore," said Justin. "That heron taking off should have helped him find us." He turned, and dashed for the forest. Jackie ran after him.

Nick hesitated. He looked out toward the water, then back into the forest. A muffled voice sounded from the lake. That made his decision a lot easier. "Hey you guys, wait for me!" he called, and ran up the path.

The three friends stood side by side under the cover of the evergreen trees at the edge of the clearing. The lighthouse appeared so close. Yet with an invisible creature lurking somewhere out there just waiting to strike any intruder, it seemed very far away. A strategy was worked out in whispers.

"There's no *kek-kek-kek* sound," said Justin. "The bird must not know we're here yet. Let's go for it."

Nick pushed him a little from behind. "You first," he said.

"No, we go together," said Jackie. "Why warn the goshawk we're here."

"What goshawk?" asked Justin. "You guys are sure scared about something that doesn't even exist."

"All right, Justin, you made your point," said Jackie. "Are we going or not?"

They heard a branch snap somewhere behind them among the trees.

"All right," Justin said. "On three. Ready?"

They nodded.

Justin counted. "One... Two... THREE!"

Side by side the three friends bolted from underneath their evergreen cover and sprinted directly at the lighthouse. The only sound was the bottom of their sneakers against the soft earth. Jackie made it inside the leaning structure first. Then Justin. And finally, Nick.

"Now what?" asked Jackie. "This is the first place that man will look for us."

Justin turned to peer out one of the many small holes in the lighthouse wall. "I hope so," he said.

"I don't get it," said Nick. He was still breathing hard. "You really want him to find us?"

"Shhhh, I think I see something," said Justin. "The branches are moving near our path."

"I hate this," Jackie said. "What do you see?"

Nick stood next to her in the darkness, waiting for Justin's moment by moment report. "Maybe it's just a deer," he said, still hoping the large man had simply given up and gone away.

"Here it comes," Justin said. "It's a... it's a..." Nick and Jackie held their breath. "It's a... spaceman?"

"A what?" Nick and Jackie asked, together. They had to see for themselves and crowded around Justin in search of their own small observation hole in the decaying wall.

They huddled together and watched as a large figure wearing a white helmet with a full tinted face mask and bulky jacket emerged cautiously into the clearing. The figure stepped forward revealing the rest of its unusual uniform – dark green rubber waders.

"Come on," whispered Justin. "Come on."

Nick was distraught. "Why do you want the bubble head to come right at us?" he asked.

Justin was irritated. "I'm not telling *him* to come on," he said. "I'm telling the goshawk."

Jackie sighed, but never removed her eye from her lookout spot. "What if the bird is already gone? We haven't heard a peep from it yet."

The large figure moved slowly toward the light-house, pausing each few steps to glance left and right.

"This had better work," said Justin. Now there was panic in his voice.

The figure took several more steps toward them, and stopped. Two large arms reached up to remove the helmet.

"If there's not a head under there, I'm screaming," said Nick.

There was a head. A regular head.

"It's him," said Justin. "It's him."

"There's that smile again," said Jackie.

Nick groaned. "We're goners."

kek-kek-kek-kek-kek-kek-kek-kek-kek.

They were familiar with the sound, but it still sent shivers down their spines.

"Here it comes," said Justin.

The large man raised his arm and hunched to absorb the impact, but it was already too late. The goshawk swooped down with its talons extended. The man cried out and fell hard to the ground.

"Let's go," said Justin.

The three Adirondack kids squeezed quickly through the opening in the lighthouse wall, sprinted for the herd path and dashed back to the boat. Jackie was first, but this time Justin and Nick tied for second.

Dax hadn't moved. She was still secure in the boat, partially hidden under the life jacket.

"Let's shove off," commanded Jackie, and grabbed the bow.

The three friends pushed the putt-putt into the water and splashed along its side, soaking their sneakers and legs all the way up to the bottoms of their shorts. They continued to lift their knees high and sloshed through the water quickly with hands guiding the boat. The exercise became harder as the

The goshawk swooped down
with its talons extended.

water became deeper, even though the boat became weightless, now suspended on the surface. They finally managed to glide the vessel through the small opening under the branches leading back out into the cove.

Jackie pulled herself up over the side and tumbled into the boat. "Come on," she said, and reached out to help Justin up alongside her.

The water reached Nick's waist. "Don't forget I've got a hole in my life jacket," he said. "Help me up."

As Justin pulled his friend safely aboard, Jackie jumped to her seat at the stern and pulled the start up cord. The engine erupted to life. "First time," she said, and smiled.

Justin and Nick cheered.

They cut quickly through the water and motored past the man's large motor boat, still anchored in the shallow cove. Nick saluted the empty craft as they sped by. "So long bubble head," he said.

Then they were in the channel, and off for home.

chapter thirteen

The Lost Lighthouse

Justin sat on his bed which had finally been placed back onto the sleeping porch. He surveyed the new wall and peered out the new screens. There was a better view outside the window with the tree that had done all the damage now gone. He noticed the wind had picked up making the water out on the lake choppy. The tops of the remaining trees in the yard bent slightly in the heavy breeze. *There are no trees close enough to reach me now*, he thought. A gallon of white primer sat on the floor in the opposite corner of the room. If it weren't for the sweet smell of new lumber, and lack of paint on the ceiling and wall, it would be hard to tell anything had happened to his favorite room at camp at all.

Dax lay curled up in a ball in a small pile of clothes stacked on the straight back wooden chair next to the bed. "I sure hope they catch that guy that keeps following us, Daxy," Justin said, and picked up the old journal that laid next to him on the bedspread. "I'm glad Mom and Dad know all about him and the lighthouse now." He reached out and buried his fingertips into the fur around Dax's chest and neck. She purred. "If they catch him, we can fish and explore and not have to worry anymore."

The phone rang downstairs. *Is it Jackie?* he thought. *Is it Nick? Mom's not calling. It must not be for me. Wait.* His heart began pounding. *Maybe they caught the guy from the lighthouse...*

Ten minutes went by and he began to relax. Then... "Justin, can you come down here?" It was his mom.

"Yes, Mom," he said. "I'm coming." He nervously set the journal back on the bed and ran down the stairs.

"And would you bring that old book with you, please?" she called.

He had just reached the bottom of the stairs, did an about face, and ran back up again. He scooped up the journal and ran back down. He was nearly at the bottom step when his mom called again. "Oh, and bring those dirty clothes from the chair, too," she said.

Justin sighed, turned, and used the railing to drag himself back up the stairs to collect his dirty shirts and shorts. "Anything else, Mom?" he called, before descending the stairs again.

"No." He began to walk. "Yes." He stopped. "Oh, no, it can wait," she finally said.

Justin hustled down the stairs, dumped his dirty clothes into the laundry room and dashed into the family room where his mom and dad were waiting. He jumped into an overstuffed chair across from them. "So, who called?" he asked. "Did they catch the guy that was following us?"

"It was Miss Holmes, the historian, returning our call," said Mrs. Robert.

Justin looked surprised. "Did she know the guy? Did she tell Ranger Bill who he is?"

"She didn't call about the man in the boat at all," said Mrs. Robert. "She called about that old journal."

"And about the lighthouse you kids found," said Mr. Robert. He sounded serious.

Justin clutched the book tightly. "Am I in some kind of trouble?" he asked, slowly.

Mr. Robert laughed. "No," he said, reassuringly. "Actually, this is pretty exciting news."

There was a knock at the door. It was Jackie and Nick.

"Good timing, you two," said Mr. Robert. "We just received an interesting call."

"Did they catch old bubble head?" asked Nick. He looked at Mr. and Mrs. Robert. "Um, are we in trouble?"

"Let's just sit down and listen," said Jackie.

Mrs. Robert explained. "Based on your discovery and on information recorded in the journal, Miss Holmes did some research and made some phone calls. Apparently you three have found the lost lighthouse written about in some of the old local history books – a lighthouse no one knew for sure even existed."

"That's what Captain McBride told me," said Justin. "If it is the old lighthouse, it could even be a hundred years old."

"That's right," said Mrs. Robert. "The property the lighthouse is on belonged to a silent film star from the 1920's. She bought the land and never even visited the Adirondacks – that land has remained undeveloped for all these years."

"It must have been hard being a movie star that couldn't even talk," said Nick.

Jackie shook her head. "The movie stars could speak," she said. "But the early movies didn't have any sound. Haven't you ever seen a silent movie before?"

"Nope, and hope I never do," said Nick. "Bor-ing."

Mrs. Robert continued. "There is no doubt that the journal is about President Harrison. And the man who drew the picture probably wrote the entries. His name was Ira Church and he was one of the president's personal guides."

"We thought he wrote, 'Chuck'," said Justin. "Like I told Miss Holmes, it was hard to make out all the words."

Nick's head jerked forward and his eyes widened. "He's probably the one that cooked the president frogs for breakfast," he said, and pointed a thumb to his chest. "If I were the president, I would have fired him."

"Here's the hard part," said Mr. Robert. Justin bit his lower lip and braced himself for the bad news. "The family that inherited the property has given the historical society permission to salvage anything they want from the lighthouse, including the journal."

Justin lowered his head and looked at the old

book. "That's okay," he said. "At least it will be safe there and a lot of people will be able to see it." He gently brushed his fingertips across the cover. "It's kind of falling apart anyway."

Nick chimed in. "And that means old bubble head won't be able to steal any of the valuable stuff that's in the lighthouse."

"But that still doesn't explain how the lighthouse ended up in the middle of the woods," Jackie said.

"There is one theory so far," said Mr. Robert. "Miss Holmes said it is possible that a storm, just like the one that struck here earlier this week, may have picked up a portion of the lighthouse from somewhere along the shore and dropped it in the woods exactly the way you found it."

"That's what we thought listening to all the storm stories at the cafe the other day," said Justin.

"This is just weird," said Nick.

There was another knock on the door and Justin jumped up to answer it. He swung the door open, looked up and froze.

A large man stood in the doorway, the wind blowing harder and the sky growing darker behind him. It was a very large man – with a very large bandage on his head.

chapter fourteen

Face to Face

Before Justin could speak, Ranger Bill Buck bounded up the porch steps alongside the stranger in the doorway. "Hello, Justin," he said, and smiled. "Are your folks at home?"

Justin could only nod. He backed away from the front door and led the two men into the family room.

"Hey, it's old bubble – I mean, it's the guy from the lighthouse," said Nick. He joined Justin and Jackie who were now sitting closer to Mr. and Mrs. Robert.

"Please have a seat," said Mr. Robert.

The two men sat down and Ranger Bill removed his forest green baseball cap. He gestured toward the man with the bandage on his head. "Well folks, I'd like to introduce Mr. Birchman," he said. "He was easy enough to locate – I found him at the medical center in Old Forge getting that nasty head wound tended to."

"Why were you following us?" asked Justin. He was surprised at his own boldness, but it was a little easier to have courage sitting so close to his parents.

Ranger Bill paused. "I think there's been some

misunderstanding here," he said. "I'll let Mr. Birchman explain."

For the first time the Adirondack kids heard the voice of the large man that had been pursuing them at the historical society and across the lake and through the woods. He smiled. "I am an amateur ornithologist," he said.

"So you wanted to fix our teeth?" blurted Nick. "You must need patients really, really bad to chase them around the lake. I don't even have a single cavity – see?" He grinned to bare his white and perfect teeth.

Mrs. Robert corrected him. "Not an orthodontist," she said. "He is an ornithologist – a person who studies birds." She looked at Mr. Birchman. "Please continue. Nicholas won't interrupt again." She gently patted Nick's shoulder and he took the hint.

Mr. Birchman continued. "When we were at the museum I was sure I heard you describe my bird of specialty – the Northern Goshawk. I have been study- ing this magnificent species for more than 25 years and I am licensed to own specimens." He pulled a long feather from his pocket, and handed it to Justin. "Just look at the size of this single tail feather."

Justin was still too nervous to examine the feather closely. "So you weren't after us to get our book?" Justin said.

"Or to steal the stuff in the old lighthouse?" said Nick.

"Oh, no, no," said Mr. Birchman. "I heard one of

you mention a lighthouse and when I learned there was only one in this entire part of the Adirondacks, I decided to camp near it on Algier Island to keep an eye out for the goshawk. When I saw all of you out on the lake I could not believe my luck. I was only hoping you could show me the place where you found the bird, so I could add the nesting site to my maps. I am so sorry you misunderstood my intentions."

"Mr. Birchman said one of you three even waved to him out on the channel," Ranger Bill said.

Nick grimaced. "That would be me," he said. "I'm the one that waved."

Jackie blushed and looked at Justin. She wasn't really comfortable yelling at him in front of his parents, but her glare spoke more than any words. Her eyes said, "I told you so."

Justin looked away from her. "It's really my fault," he said. "I'm the one that got kind of carried away with the whole bad guy thing." He looked at Mr. Birchman's head and remembered the terrible gash on Nick's life jacket. "I'm really sorry the goshawk got you."

Mr. Birchman laughed. "Oh, this is not your fault at all," he said. "I should have known better. I am certainly aware of what the goshawk is capable of when it still has its offspring around. They are very protective of their young."

Justin looked at his parents. *Just like my mom and dad*, he thought, and finally he was able to smile.

chapter fifteen

A Tiger by the Tail

Justin, Jackie and Nick stood on the Robert's dock, their shirts and shorts billowing in the wind.

"I'm sorry, Jackie," said Justin. "I know how important winning that fishing contest was to you."

Jackie shrugged. "It's no big deal," she said. "I think I'll head over to the island before the water gets much rougher. It looks like it might storm again soon."

Nick pointed. "There's still stuff floating in the lake from the last storm," he said. "Look at that big stick coming this way."

"That's not a stick," said Jackie. She was already headed to the putt-putt for her gear. "That's a Tiger Muskie."

"Moby Dick is back?" said Nick. He ran after Jackie.

"Grab my pole for me," said Justin. He dashed into the boat house for their live bait.

The three friends reunited on the dock, plunged their hands into the pail for their minnows and within seconds cast their lines into the direction of the gigantic fish's last known location.

Plop... plop... plop. Three lines out. Three bob-bers splashing onto the choppy surface of the water.

They sat and watched the little red and white bulbs that danced playfully over and around in the waves. Their motion had an almost hypnotic affect. Seconds seemed like minutes. Minutes seemed like hours.

"Where did that fish go?" asked Justin.

"We were so lucky last time," said Jackie. "I can't believe we are getting a second chance."

Nick was in the middle of a yawn when he was suddenly jarred back to reality by the zing of the line quickly disappearing from his reel.

"Hey, where's your bobber?" asked Justin.

"Set the hook," yelled Jackie. "Set the hook *now.*"

Nick was startled. He tried to stand up and fell backward. The pole slipped from his hands.

"Oh, no you don't," said Jackie. She pounced on the reel before it reached the edge of the dock. "I hope you set the hook."

There was an eruption in the water as nearly four feet of prehistoric-looking creature shot straight up out of the lake writhing in the air. It seemed to soar above the tree line of Cedar Island that stretched out in front of them before gravity brought its huge dark body back down with a loud smack into the water again. White spray shot up marking the spot where the mammoth fish had reentered its deep and

There was an eruption in the water
as nearly four feet of prehistoric-looking
creature shot straight up out of the lake,
writhing in the air.

dark domain.

"Yes," said Jackie, excitedly. "I'd say the hook is set all right."

"Please don't howl again," said Nick.

The battle between Jackie and the giant fish raged on. There were more spectacular jumps and fishing line coming in and going out. Justin felt himself tire just from watching.

"I'm bringing it in," said Jackie. "I can't believe it. This muskie feels even bigger than the one out by Algier Island. Get the net ready."

Nick ran to the putt-putt and returned with net in hand. He dropped to his knees at the edge of the dock to reach out and scoop up the fish. "Come on, Moby," he said. "Captain Ahab is waiting for you." There was a swell in the water in front of him and a large gaping mouth lined with razor sharp teeth emerged from the foam. He screamed and the net dropped into the lake. It was knocked away by the fish churning about in the water for its life.

"Great, Nick, now we have to slide it up onto the dock," said Jackie.

Justin could tell she was getting really tired, but her determination inspired him. He stood alongside her to grip the pole and together they pulled. The dock shook as the fish banged against it. Nick joined in and the three pulled again. The giant fish kicked with its tail and actually aided in its slide up onto the dock where it continued to flip and flop uncontrollably in every direction.

Nick stepped back. "Now what do we do with it?" he asked.

Jackie had already charged in on it. "We pick it up," she said.

Justin hesitated. "I'm not getting near the head," he said.

"I'll lift it," said Jackie. "You two grab the middle and the tail."

"I think you may have won the contest with this one," Justin said, as he moved slowly toward the fish.

Nick tried to hold the tail, but the fish slapped him with it. "What do you mean," he said. The fish slapped him again. "I caught it. And then it almost bit my whole face right off. I should win something."

"Don't even start," said Jackie.

"Hey Dad," Justin called.

"Why are you calling him?" asked Nick.

"To take a picture for the menu at the Tamarack Cafe," said Justin.

The three slowly lifted the fish. All of them groaned from the great weight of it.

"This thing is almost as long as the whole wing span of the goshawk," said Justin. "Maybe even longer." He looked over at Jackie as she firmly held the long steel leader that was so close to the muskie's razor sharp teeth. The sinister mouth of the fish appeared locked in the shape of a mock grin. Justin winced as he looked at the large unblinking eye that stared up at him. "You really aren't afraid of anything are you, Jackie?"

"Not really," Jackie said.

"Except that huge spider on her foot," said Nick.

"What?" Jackie panicked and the steel leader slipped from her grasp.

The sudden shift in weight caused Justin to lose his grip as well, leaving Nick with his hands left on the slippery tail. The fish smacked against the dock as Nick fell down with it in a desperate attempt to hold on, but to no avail. The Tiger Muskie took full advantage of the opportunity and with another jerk, bounced on the dock, spit out the hook and splashed back into the lake.

Moby Dick was free.

The only solid evidence remaining of the catch was the fishy scent left on their hands.

Mr. Robert appeared at the top of the sloping lawn with Dax trotting along at his side. "What's all the excitement about?" he asked as they approached the dock. He looked into their faces. "Are you three all right?"

"We caught a Tiger Muskie, Dad," said Justin. "Well, Nick did at first. But really it was Jackie. Anyway, we wanted you to take a picture of it."

"I see," Mr. Robert said. He glanced around. "Where is it?"

Dax was already investigating the scene and was sniffing all about the dock everywhere as she moved.

"It sort of got away," said Nick. "But you should have seen it, Mr. Robert, it was gigantic. I'll bet it weighed 100 pounds. And it almost bit my face right off. We really did catch it. Here – you can even smell my hands."

"No, that's okay Nick," said Mr. Robert.

"It was really big, Dad," said Justin. "It didn't have a red tag on it, but it would have won the trophy for the biggest fish for sure. Look, we can show you where it bounced on the dock."

It was too late. Dax had walked all through any impressions left by the flopping fish. Any distinct shape left by Moby Dick on the dock now looked like simple puddles of water.

"Well, if you catch it again call me, and I'll be glad to take a picture," said Mr. Robert. He turned to walk back to the cabin. "Justin, dinner is in about fifteen minutes, okay?"

"Yes, Dad, thanks," said Justin. He looked at Jackie who was still silent. With her blonde hair blowing in the wind and her hands in her pockets she just continued to look out at the lake. He couldn't believe she wasn't screaming or crying or strangling Nick or something.

"It doesn't matter that the muskie got away," she said. "It doesn't matter that we didn't win the contest. And it doesn't matter that our picture won't be in the menu at the Tamarack Cafe. And it doesn't even matter if Justin's dad doesn't really believe we caught that fish."

"It doesn't?" said Nick.

"No, it doesn't," said Jackie. She turned and looked at both of them. "We know that we caught the biggest fish in Fourth Lake. And we'll know that for the rest of our lives. That's all that matters."

Nick looked relieved.

Justin wondered at her. She was often bossy and acting like she was their mother. But this was different somehow. All he knew is that it was the most grown up thing he had ever heard her say.

epilogue

Justin sat on the porch with his sketch book in his lap and held the goshawk feather by its pointed tip between the forefinger and thumb of his left hand. He leaned his head back on his Adirondack chair and held the feather up in front of him. It was nearly as long as Dax's entire tail, mostly gray and accented with broad brown horizontal bands. The tip was white.

He had tried to draw pictures of his friends, but without success. The crumpled sheets of paper on the porch floor bore the evidence of his many failures. Maybe he would never draw at all!

But maybe he could draw this feather.

As he moved his pencil on the paper, he thought about his friends.

This feather is like Jackie. It's thin and light, but its really strong.

He drew some more.

And its kind of like my friendship with Nick. Even if it gets all ruffled, somehow a high five or a stupid joke seems to smooth it back into the right shape again.

He turned the feather over in his hand and continued to study it carefully.

He drew some more.

But how is this feather like me?

He set his pencil down and holding the feather from each end, slowly tried to bend it. He could feel the stress on the shaft. It was definitely flexible. But he also knew if he pulled too hard, it could snap.

That's kind of like me. Bendable. But not invincible.

Then he remembered Mr. Birchman had said that when a bird loses a feather, it can always grow a new one to replace it.

He looked at the feather. Then down at his drawing.

Maybe I can do this after all, he thought. *Maybe I really can.*

And he drew some more.

DAX FACTS

The **Northern Goshawk** is a hawk of the forest. Its three and a half foot wing span and long agile tail help the large gray bird of prey move quickly and accurately through the trees.

Northern Goshawks are very protective of their young and will sound the *kek-kek-kek* alarm call when disturbed and even attack intruders.

In the Adirondacks, goshawk nests are made of large sticks which are located 30 to 40 feet high in white pine or yellow birch trees. It is important to avoid goshawk nests completely when adults are hatching their eggs so they won't abandon them.

Photograph ©2003 appears courtesy Jim Spencer and Dave Armstong

The Northern Goshawk swoops in on an intruder to protect its young.

Photograph ©2003 appears courtesy Jim Spencer and Dave Armstong
The Northern Goshawk

Photographs appear by permission of the President Benjamin Harrison Home, Indianapolis, IN.

President Benjamin Harrison

🐾 DAX FACTS

Benjamin Harrison was the 23rd President of the United States. He was elected in 1888 and served from 1889 to 1893. He was named for his great grandfather, a signer of the Declaration of Independence. His grandfather, William Henry Harrison, was 9th President of the United States.

The Harrisons were the first family to have a decorated Christmas tree in the White House. The President also conducted Bible studies in the White House and during his administration the practice of displaying the American Flag over the White House and all public buildings was begun.

In 1896, the Harrison family built their summer retreat on Second Lake near Old Forge in the Adirondack Mountains. They called it Berkeley Lodge. The twin tower cottage designed and built by architect Charles E. Cronk, is now a private residence. The camp also had a boat house and a house for guides. The President loved the Adirondacks where he enjoyed boating, fishing, hunting and relaxing with his family.

President and Mrs. Benjamin Harrison at Berkeley Lodge on Second Lake near Old Forge in the Adirondack Mountains of New York State.

To learn more about President Benjamin Harrison contact President Benjamin Harrison Home, 1230 North Delaware Street, Indianapolis, IN 46202-2598.

🐱✒️ DAX FACTS

The 25 foot tall **Shoal Point Lighthouse** on Fourth Lake in the Adirondacks was built in the late 1800's and sits on the north shore across from the western tip of Algier Island.

The old lighthouse was falling into disrepair and was restored in 2001 under the leadership of the Fourth Lake Property Owners' Association. Once believed lit at night by a kerosene lantern, today the lighthouse shines with a rotating airport landing beacon.

A 16 foot mystery lighthouse on Fourth Lake is mentioned in the local history, *Up Old Forge Way,* but to date there is no evidence to support its existence. There are a few lighthouses on Lake Champlain, but no others on the interior lakes of the Adirondacks.

An early 1900s penny postcard of Shoal Point Lighthouse on Fourth Lake in the Adirondacks.

About the Authors

Gary and Justin VanRiper are a father and son writing team residing in Camden, New York of the Tug Hill region along with their family and cats, Socks and Dax. They spend many summer and autumn days at camp on Fourth Lake in the Adirondacks.

The Adirondack Kids™ began as a short writing exercise when Justin was in third grade. Encouraged after a public reading of an early draft at a Parents As Reading Partners (PARP) program in the Camden Central School District, the project grew into a middle reader chapter book series. *The Adirondack Kids #3* is their third book.

About the Illustrators

Glenn Guy is an award-winning political cartoonist who lives in Canastota, New York. *The Adirondack Kids #3* is his third book.

Susan Loeffler is a freelance illustrator who lives and works in Camden, New York. *The Adirondack Kids #3* is her third book.